THE BUNNY BUNCH FAMILY
by Sunny Griffin

Illustrated by Esther Kennedy

Papa Bunny is big and strong.

He works in the garden all day long.

ama Bunny
is busy as
can be.

She cooks
and feeds
our family.

Sister Bunny
draws and
paints each
day. . .

She goes to school to learn and to play.

Brother Bunny rides his bike to school. . .

Every day he goes to the Bunnyville swimming pool.

Baby Bunny
is held and
loved by
everyone. . .

He eats and sleeps and has lots of fun.

Grandma and Grandpa Bunny are special, too. . .

So come and visit...

...we all like *you!*